CW00859671

2

Many years ago, a STEAM castle was built in a remote area of STEAM Valley. It's a far-away place to help children continue developing their skills in Science, Technology, Engineering, Arts, and Mathematics.

These children, with their parents and assigned educators, have fun learning! They explore problems that deal with communicating, improving products, testing, planning, asking questions, creating, imagining, exploring, and planning.

The STEAM castle was built to teach children how to help the world become a better place. These children are crucial to the world's future advancements.

Meanwhile, things are not so great in STEAM Valley. Let's take a look!

4

One early morning, Miss Knowledge, the STEAM Master's assistant, burst into the STEAM Master's room in fright, yelling at the top of her lungs with all her might!

The STEAM children are declining like a thief in the night. This will cause us problems if we don't reach a solution before midnight.

The STEAM Master quickly rose
out of his bed with delight, stating to
Miss. Knowledge, "No worries. It'll
be alright."

Miss Knowledge, with her head sunk low, decided she must go. As she walked out the door, she said, "If we don't fix this problem before midnight, the STEAM program will dissolve faster than the speed of light."

The STEAM Master then jumped out of bed and said, "Miss Knowledge, can we fix this problem tonight, before we unleash a disaster on the world that will cause much fright?"

Miss Knowledge quickly said, "We can make this problem alright, if we can quickly contact Dribbles, Nicky, Ricky, and Blicky tonight."

Miss Knowledge said softly with delight, "Dribbles and Friends are the solution we need to correct this problem before we all go to bed tonight."

The STEAM Master said, "Alright! Contact Dribbles and Friends while I prepare the STEAM bus for flight."

The STEAM Master buckled up for flight ... then quickly set the course for Pleasant Valley by saying, "Alright. We need to find Dribbles and Friends before midnight."

13

The STEAM bus hopped and popped with all its might, while flying into the sky, just like a rocket ship that could EASILY blast off to the moon in flight.

What seemed like a trip that would last ten nights, the STEAM bus only took them two minutes to get there ... once in flight.

When the STEAM Master saw Pleasant Valley in sight, he pulled the bright red lever, landing the bus with all his might! Afterwards, he smiled with great delight.

15

The STEAM Master
jumped out of the bus to see
countless children playing
in the streets.

16

He then looked around a big, blue tree, as he started to walk faster, puffing constantly.

The STEAM Master walked
towards a big yellow tree
that was shaped like a
beautiful Honeybee.

18

He scratched his head because
he didn't know what to do.
The big yellow Honeybee tree
then said, "If you're looking for
Dribbles and Friends, you need
to walk straight ahead."

The STEAM Master was
amazed to see a big, yellow
Honeybee tree speaking
so eloquently.

Dribbles and Friends Straight Ahead

He walked a little further and came across a sign that said, "Dribbles and Friends straight ahead."

Startled and amazed, he picked up his pace.

When the STEAM Master got a little closer, he was utterly amazed. That's because Dribbles and Friends were walking around teaching children how to comprehend Science, Technology, Engineering, Arts and Mathematics completely unfazed.

Dribbles and Friends looked up to see the STEAM Master was approaching them as fast as can be.

That's when they reached out and hugged him happily!

Dribbles then said to the STEAM Master with absolute fright, "How's Miss Knowledge doing? Is she uptight? hear everything in STEAM Valley is no alright."

The STEAM Master said, "You're absolutely right. That's why we have to move faster than the speed of light! We need to save STEAM Valley before the clock strikes midnight."

He proclaimed, "The STEAM program is quickly losing children, and that's not right."

Dribbles then said, "No need to be uptight. All the children here are bright. Their parents have taught them since birth to understand Science, Technology, Engineering, Arts and Mathematics ... and to always be polite."

The STEAM Master was eager to see if the children understood the basics of STEAM willingly.

25

Dribbles and Friends took him to see a huge golden castle where the children were taught Science, Technology, Engineering, Arts and Mathematics constantly.

They approached the castle cautiously, to be greeted by a gold "talking" tree that welcomed them gleefully!

28

Dribbles then said with much delight, "These children study STEAM projects both day and night."

He added, "The key is to teach children early in life not to waste their time in senseless arguments and fights."

Blicky chimed in with a grin and stressed, "Education is alright! The more you learn, the greater impact it can have on your life."

30

Ricky scratched his head and said, "I agree. This STEAM journey is absolutely the right fit for me."

Nicky smiled and said, "No matter who you are or what people say, never let a STEAM possibility discourage you in ANY WAY."

She added, "There are educators out there who will help you all the way through! Never lose sight of the advantages STEAM programs can have for you!"

Everyone then walked into the castle to see a room full of children working effortlessly.

The STEAM Master looked on with delight, while reminding Dribbles and Friends they had to return to Steam Valley by the stroke of midnight.

Dribbles and Friends said, "Aright! We'll get you back to the STEAM bus with the parents and children so we can take flight."

The STEAM Master smiled with amazing delight and said to everyone there, "Will that be alright?"

The children and their parents were very polite and said, "Let's go back to STEAM Valley to correct the problem that's in sight."

They all rushed to the STEAM bus like birds in flight. It was a miracle because they arrived at STEAM Valley before the clock struck midnight.

Miss Knowledge met them at the door, as the stars glistened in the night. She tucked each child in bed and said, "The STEAM program will now be alright! Everyone in the world can sleep well tonight."

Printed by BoD˘in Norderstedt, Germany